PRETORIA

HANNESBURG

Mozambique

Swaziland

Lesotho

N

DURBAN

ZABETH

AFRICA

CFS

For more information about the Save Our Seas Foundation,
please visit our website at
www.SaveOurSeas.com

Book designed and packaged by Jokar Productions, LLC

For information regarding permission, write to Save Our Seas Foundation,
Attention: Permissions Department, 6 rue Bellot, 1206 Geneva, Switzerland

ISBN 978-0-9800444-0-9

©2008 Jokar Productions, LLC
Photography/Tom Campbell

10 9 8 7 6 5 4 3 2 1

Printed in China

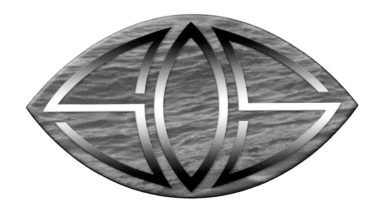

THE GREAT WHITE RED ALERT

by Geoffrey T. Williams

Photography/Tom Campbell

Illustrated by
Artful Doodlers

save our seas
FOUNDATION

THE GREAT WHITE RED ALERT

One

Face Off

The emergency alert came at a bad time.

Of course, there's never a *good* time to find out someone is destroying the ocean in some far-flung corner of the world. But, for Alena, the timing couldn't have been worse.

The great white shark could have told you...

* * * * *

The twins, Alena and Tyler Worthy, had taken their big hydroplane, the *Sea Worthy*, across the Santa Barbara Channel to San Miguel Island for a Saturday of diving and research.

Tyler parked the boat between Point Bennet and Castle Rock at the western tip of the island. A light breeze was clearing the early morning fog. It was going to be a warm day. Tyler looked around, grinning.

"We're going to have lots of company in the water," he said.

The beach and rocks were almost invisible beneath the shiny, squirming bodies of thousands of pinnipeds—commonly known as seals and sea lions. The water around the boat was dotted with dark heads bobbing up and down as they hunted breakfast.

"Are we taking the *Nous Venons?*" Tyler asked his sister. *Nous venons* is French for "we're coming," and was the name of their small, sleek, and very fast personal submarine, currently stowed below, in the large hold of the hydroplane.

"No. Just the scuba tanks," Alena replied. "I just need to get some kelp and bottom samples."

"Great," Tyler said. "I'll shoot some video to update the website."

In case you're wondering why two high school kids have a hydroplane, a personal submarine, and other very special equipment, it's easy enough to explain: it was all supplied by the Save Our Seas Foundation. The twins are two of the three members of the S.O.S. Foundation's Aquatic Intervention (A.I.) Team. It was their job to stop terrible things from happening in the world's oceans.

The team's third member was currently yipping, yapping, barking along with the seals, and acting just about as excited as a Jack Russell terrier can act. Brutus was his name. He'd been with the team since he was a puppy and figured he was half-fish, so he was anxious to get in the water with the twins.

"Sorry, Brutus," Alena said. "Not this time."

Alena made dive decisions for the team because she was older than Tyler—by nearly six minutes—a fact she rarely let her brother forget. She also had more diving hours than the others. Brutus, of course, had the fewest, and most of his were inside the *Nous Venons* where they didn't need breathing units. He had growled and bared his teeth the only time Tyler had tried to fit him with scuba gear. The little fins were okay, but the tiny mask pinched his ears and slanted his eyes until he looked like a crazy Siamese cat. After some serious jumping and face licking, Brutus got Tyler to promise to fix it. A few hours in the A.I. lab, and Tyler had fabricated a fully-enclosed diving setup that was comfortable for the dog.

"You think we'll find any problems down there?" Tyler asked.

"Well, *those* things are still here." Alena said, pointing to a couple of oil platforms several kilometers away. "I want to see if the tanker traffic has affected the pinnipeds." An important part of the A.I. Team's job was checking for environmental damage in the Channel Islands National Park. When there were problems, the oil platforms were number one on their list of suspects.

As the twins finished dressing for the dive, Brutus whined some more about having to stay behind.

Tyler knelt, scratching the dog's neck. "You're just about snack-size for those sea lions. Besides, *someone* has to stay here in case of an emergency."

Brutus wasn't buying it, but seemed to resign himself to surface duty.

After carefully checking each other's gear, the twins rolled off the diving platform, sliding into the blue-green silence.

Tyler was slightly below and behind Alena, guiding the high-definition camera and lights on a small power-sled. Alena checked her mask displays. The readouts told her the depth and distance to the *Sea Worthy*, her GPS location to within a meter anywhere on Earth, the amount of time she had been down, and air remaining in her scuba tank. All readouts were normal.

Alena spoke into the wi-pad microphone. "Don't get separated." Tyler had designed the team's wireless, personnel audio devices, and the underwater communication system sounded as good as her MP3 player. "And keep a lookout for sharks."

Not that Tyler needed the reminder: the water between Castle Rock and Point Bennet wasn't called Shark Park for nothing, and the twins had seen shortfin makos, blues, and even great whites on many dives. They loved the animals; their beauty and grace were thrilling to watch—from a cautious distance.

Alena was swimming toward the edge of a forest of giant kelp when it happened.

The seaweed was weaving gently back and forth, like folds in a tall curtain. The sunlight above made dramatic streamers of light and shadow through the thick leaves.

Then, presto-change-o, just like magic, the shadows shifted and Alena found herself face to face with a great white shark!

She stopped swimming, watching the shark, its powerful tail slowly moving from side to side. She wasn't afraid. Sharks don't usually pay much attention to divers unless provoked or threatened, and this one wasn't paying attention to her at all.

Until the emergency alert went off.

The inside of her mask began pulsing with a bright red glow at the same time a computerized voice sounded in her earbuds. *"AI Code Red. This is not a drill. Repeat. This is not a drill. This is an AI Code Red."*

One of the S.O.S. satellites had picked up a signal from somewhere in the world and relayed it to the *Sea Worthy*. Brutus, who was very smart and well trained, had immediately pawed a switch on the ship's console to forward the signal to the twins. He did exactly the right thing. At exactly the wrong time.

Fumbling for a button on her wrist, Alena quickly turned off the alert.

Too late—the shark was looking straight at her. She could see rows of razor-edged teeth. She had to fight the natural urge to move backwards knowing this could very well trigger the action she wanted to avoid. Trying hard to stay vertical in the water since anything horizontal would look like most of the shark's prey, she made sure not to be mistaken for a large seal. That would not be good.

She kept her eyes fixated on the 1000-kilo predator less than 3 meters away from her. Now 2 meters away.

Now one.

Now…

After what seemed like an eternity to the girl, but was really no more than a few seconds, the white seemed to shrug off the momentary irritation. It flicked its long tail, the surge pushing Alena away. Within moments it was a dim shape in the distance.

"Wow," Tyler's voice sounded in her ear. "I got it. I got all of it. That was way cool. Wait'll I post that on the website!"

"Way cool. Yeah." Alena let out a breath she hadn't realized she'd been holding. "Glad we could put on a show for you, little brother." Then, a moment later, she said, "Come on. We have to check out the alert."

They began swimming to the surface. What neither of them mentioned, but both were thinking was *will we respond to the alert in time?* Too many times the A.I. Team had arrived too late to do anything but help clean up another mess. Would this time be different?

TWO

SHARK FIN SOUP

Tyler sat in the flight deck of the *Sea Worthy*. That's right: the *flight* deck. The hydroplane had transformed into a large, very fast jet plane—with just the push of a couple of buttons. The team was now flying at 1000 kilometers per hour at an altitude of 10,000 meters toward Cape Town, South Africa where the alert had originated.

They had taken off from San Miguel Island shortly after getting back aboard the boat from their dive.

While Tyler prepared for their twenty-hour flight to the other side of the world, Alena v-mailed their parents, letting them know where they were going, and when they might return. Another v-mail to school arranged for online classes—no sense missing a biology midterm. She checked the *Nous Venons*, tucked snugly in the hold, then the cupboards and the refrigerator, deciding they could put up with veggie burgers and salads while they were in the air. She grinned when she saw there was an unopened box of *Walker's Stem Ginger Biscuits* on a shelf. The twins always fought over who got the most of the delicious cookies. Making sure Tyler was busy, she tucked the box away in a bulkhead compartment behind a stack of lifejackets.

"This is your Captain speaking. Flight attendants prepare for take-off." Tyler liked using the intercom system.

Alena shook her head. *He thinks he's so funny.*

"And don't forget to bring that box of ginger biscuits up to the flight deck," Tyler added.

Busted by the ship's video system! Alena sighed. *It's going to be a long flight.*

* * * * *

The *Sea Worthy* was on autopilot, and the twins were getting a video update from Jakob Bheka, the S.O.S. Foundation's representative in South Africa, who had sent the alert.

"Two hundred dollars!" Tyler exclaimed. "Who pays two hundred dollars for a bowl of soup!?"

"Thoughtless people with too much money," Jakob said. His dark, serious face stared back at the twins from one of the high-definition video displays. "We had a report that jaws from a great white sold for fifty-thousand dollars." He took off his glasses to polish the lenses—something he did when he was upset or nervous. Right now he was upset, though his voice remained calm.

"But South Africa was the first country in the world to pass laws protecting white sharks. Aren't they being enforced?" asked Alena.

"They are," Jakob said, putting his glasses back on. "And the authorities stop a lot of the killing. But shark fins and jaws are still some of the most expensive animal products in the world. And remember, shark finning is a multi-million dollar industry benefiting from the sale of shark fins used in Asian soups and Chinese medicines which are more popular than ever. Especially when they're made from the fins of a great white."

"But by the time the fins are dried, bleached and dried again, they have to add chicken stock to make it taste like anything," Alena said.

Jakob sighed. "It's not the flavor they're paying for, it's the status. Just showing they can afford something that expensive."

"Last we heard the United Nations estimated over 100-million sharks are killed every year," Alena said.

"So who's doing the killing there? And how do we find them and stop them?" Tyler asked.

The quiet hiss of the plane's systems filled the silence as Jakob looked at them. Finally he said, "That's why I called you. We don't know."

THREE

RUMORS AND GUESSES

All we have right now are rumors and guesses," Jakob said.

It was twenty-four hours later. Jakob had joined the twins aboard the *Sea Worthy*. Transformed from jet back to hydrofoil, the boat was anchored outside Gansbaai harbor near the tip of Danger Point, Southeast of Cape Town, South Africa.

"Let's start with the rumors," Tyler said.

"The money's coming from Hong Kong," explained Jakob. "Some restaurants have banded together and hired a rogue captain and a crew."

"Any names?" said Alena.

"All we've heard is 'Poison Flower.'"

"Not a restaurant I'd eat at," said Tyler.

Jakob gave a small smile. "Might be the name of the ship," he suggested.

"How are they catching the sharks?" asked Alena.

"We don't even know that. But over the past month or so the cage-diving companies have found the bodies of sharks that have been finned. Up around Quoin Point, several dozen have washed up along the beach. All the great whites have been decapitated as well so their jaws can be taken and sold."

The twins were sickened by the senseless slaughter. Part of the Foundation's work is to get the world to pay attention. Sharks are not the monsters that movies try to make them. They don't breed quickly or often. Very rarely do they attack humans. When they do it's usually either a case of mistaken identity, or the human has done something foolish. Outlaw hunters, or pirates, kill many of the sharks and "fin" them. They haul the fish up on deck and cut off their fins while they're still alive. The helpless animals are not even kept for food; they're just dumped back into the sea to die. The brutal practice continues despite the fact that it has been outlawed in many countries.

"Is it happening around Dyer Island?" asked Tyler.

Dyer Island and Geyser Rock are just a few kilometers off the coast of Gansbaai and are the best spots in the world to dive with great whites. That's because Geyser Rock is home to fifty thousand or more Cape Fur seals—the favorite food for white sharks.

Jakob shook his head. "We've been patrolling up and down the coast—Cape Town to Struisbaai—and haven't spotted a thing. It's like they know we're coming."

Alena and Tyler looked at each other. "Sounds like a job for Arky," Alena said.

Tyler nodded. "I'll go wake him up." He headed down to the lab.

The *Sea Worthy's* laboratory was packed with high-tech equipment including computer-controlled machines to make just about anything (such as diving gear for a dog), a high-definition video editing system, biological and chemical analysis equipment, and a scanning electron microscope. If Tyler needed it and didn't have it, he could get it. The Foundation wanted the team to have the best equipment possible.

A large aluminum container was standing against a bulkhead. Inside was a bright titanium tube. It looked like a missile, except that it had a round top made of thick Plexiglas. Behind the Plexiglas was a camera lens. Long wings on either side were extended on takeoff. The tail looked like the tail of a small airplane. There was a control panel with lights, buttons, and an LED screen that was now dark.

Tyler pushed a button. After a moment the LED screen lit up with the words "HELLO" in bright green letters. As Tyler watched, the camera lens came to life. It swiveled, stopped, and focused on the boy. "Hello, Tyler Worthy," said a computer-generated voice.

"Hello, Arky," said Tyler. "How are you?"

"All systems. Are go," Arky said.

"We have a mission for you," said Tyler.

"Mission. Good." That was Arky's way of saying he had heard and understood.

If you haven't already guessed, Arky was pretty smart—for a machine. Arky was a nickname and much easier to say than *Autonomous Aerial Reconnaissance Craft*. The machine could be programmed to fly just about anywhere and send pictures back to the ship.

Tyler flipped a switch to open a port in the deck above. A hydraulic lift slowly raised Arky up to the deck, ready for his mission.

Four

Arky Aloft

The *Nous Venons* was cruising on the surface between Dyer Island and Geyser Rock. Nearby Geyser Rock was teeming with sea lions. Their noisy barking sounded above the quiet motor of the sub. The channel was shallow and Tyler was keeping a close eye on the depth finder as he drove. Brutus was sitting on his haunches next to Alena. His tongue hanging out of his mouth looked like a small slab of bacon. He seemed to be hypnotized by the hand sweeping around in the green face of the radar screen. Alena was busy monitoring the video Arky was sending back, looking for anything that hinted of pirates. Jakob was at the conning tower, a raised viewing area on the *Nous Venons*. He scanned the horizon with powerful binoculars.

Arky was flying 60 meters over the water, following the twisting, turning coastline, in and out of the many small bays along the way, his lens constantly swiveling and focusing. He was programmed to zoom in on any watercraft—and there were plenty: small fishing vessels, ordinary pleasure boats, and several cage-diving boats, their decks filled with excited tourists hoping to dive with great white sharks. Alena could see nothing that looked out of place. The coast was beautiful: long, empty strands of beaches, rugged cliffs, patches of shining blue water, an occasional small village, or isolated house.

"Look at those swells," she said, thinking of the beaches back home. "Wouldn't it be great to be surfing right now?"

Brutus let out an excited yelp.

"What?" Alena said.

The dog barked again, now standing, tail quivering, looking at the radar display.

"The radar!" Tyler said. He patted Brutus. "Way to go, boy."

Alena watched the hand sweep around. A large blip appeared. "It's big, whatever it is. Too far away for Arky to see." She called up to Jakob, "Jake, you see anything due east?"

Jakob focused the binoculars and scanned the sea off their starboard, or right, side. "Sea's a little rough. Hard to make out much. Wait! Something's there. Maybe eight or ten kilometers away. Might be a ship. Doesn't seem to be moving. Can we ask Arky to do a flyover?"

Alena opened a communication channel to the craft, "Arky?" she said.

"Hello, Alena Worthy."

"Hello Arky. We need to make a small change."

"Change. Good." Alena entered new instructions, and Arky veered off toward the unknown vessel.

FIVE

HOT PURSUIT

Arky was headed straight for the ship. For ship it was—they could all see it now, though it was unlike any they'd seen before.

It was over 60 meters long, painted a speckled, greenish-grey, almost like camouflage. There were several small structures near the bow. The tall command structure stood in the middle. Antennas and communication dishes sprouted like weeds at every level. At the stern, or back, were three giant coverings, over 5 meters in diameter, positioned side by side. From Arky's position, Alena couldn't tell what they were. Maybe the strangest thing about the ship was its hull: from the water up to nearly 10 meters where the deck started, the ship looked like it was floating on a bloated, round, dark *something*—like a huge inner tube, or skirt.

The *Nous Venons* was less than a kilometer away. Tyler wasn't going to risk getting any closer until they knew more.

"The *Poison Flower*?" Jakob said.

"We'll see. Arky. Circle," ordered Alena.

Arky began to circle.

"There's no name that I can see," Alena said a few minutes later. She found herself almost whispering. Something about the strange ship made her want to walk on tiptoe and cross her fingers. Arky focused on the stern of the ship and the huge coverings.

Alena finally figured out what was underneath them. "Those are giant propellers!"

"It's a hovercraft," Tyler said. "Probably a *Zubr*. Made in Russia. I've heard of them, but never seen one. I didn't know they were this big."

All of a sudden the huge vessel came to life! Antennas turned toward the *Nous Venons*. The sub's underwater microphones picked up a low *thrumming* sound, building in volume until Tyler had to turn down the speakers. Brutus jumped under the display console, shivering.

"What's happening?" Tyler said.

"Nothing good. Look," Alena said. Arky was sending back close-ups of the structures at the bow, or front, of the ship. "Guns! Deck-mounted machine guns!"

"We're outta here," Tyler said. "Hang on!" He revved up the sub's powerful engine, jamming the throttle forward and cranking the rudder hard to starboard. Like the super-sub it was, the *Nous Venons* turned on a dime and began speeding toward the coast and safety.

Jakob was watching the craft with growing dread. "This is not good," he said. "Not good at all. How fast can a *Zubr* go?"

"Sixty knots," replied Tyler.

"What's our top speed?"

Tyler looked over his shoulder, catching Alena's eye, then looked at Jakob. "Maybe twenty. On a good day."

"This is not feeling like a good day," said Jakob. But the big ship hadn't moved. "They're not coming after us yet. Maybe we don't have to worry about—"

Alena, who was still watching the video, suddenly interrupted. "Hey. Does that thing have a mouth?"

"What?" said Tyler.

"The whole front's opening up."

"Impossible," said Tyler. "Hovercrafts are built for beach landings. The front opens after they hit land. You know, to unload equipment. If they open it in the water, they'll flood."

"I guess someone forgot to tell them that," Alena said.

"Something's coming out," Jakob said.

"Arky?"

"Hello. Alena Worthy."

"Track whatever that is."

"Track. Whatever. Good."

Each sweep of the radar screen now showed the big blip of the *Zubr* and four smaller images that were heading for the *Nous Venons*.

"They're closing in," said Alena. "A thousand meters…nine hundred…." She turned to watch the video. "Arky's on them now. Oh, no! They're go-fast boats. We'll never outrun them!"

Six

Unfriendly Fire

Rooster tails of water shot up as the go-fast boats picked up speed. Smugglers often used go-fast boats because they're so low in the water that radar can't see them, and so fast that no one can catch them. The controls are at the stern so the long forward section can be used to store whatever is being smuggled.

There were three crewmen in the lead boat. They hadn't spotted Arky. They had their backs to his camera, intent on catching the *Nous Venons*.

"Five hundred meters and closing. Arky. Lower," ordered Alena.

"Lower. Good."

"Catch up to it."

"Catch. Good."

The view of the cockpit grew larger in the video display. The man at the wheel was short and wide, with a long black ponytail blown back by the wind. Another crewman was bald and had a wide belt hung with two pistols. The third crewman was taller and was wearing some kind of uniform. At least Alena thought it was a uniform. There were symbols on the back, but she couldn't make them out. Maybe Chinese.

"Two hundred meters."

Alena saw the crewmen raise a weapon to his shoulder, aiming at

the sub.

"He's got a rocket launcher!" Alena cried. "Dive! Dive!" But there was no time.

There was a burst of smoke as the man fired.

Tyler jerked the wheel sharply, throwing them all against the port bulkhead. The rocket screamed past and exploded harmlessly, sending up a fountain of seawater.

The man was reloading when he became aware of Arky behind him. The man turned around and aimed.

Alena let out a gasp.

Arky was almost on top of the go-fast boat. The man's cruel face filled the screen.

"Arky!" Alena screamed.

"Hello. Alena Wor—"

All the screens went dark.

Looking back from the conning tower, Jakob saw a bright blossom of flame as Arky crashed into the stern of the go-fast boat. The sound of the explosion came a moment later.

"They're sinking," Jakob said. "Two…no, all three men made it overboard."

"What about the other boats?" Tyler said.

Jakob scanned the scene. Smoke was rising from the ruined boat. "They're stopping. Picking up the crew."

Alena anxiously adjusted the dials on the video displays. "Arky?" she said in a soft whisper. "Arky…?"

But the screens remained dark.

SEVEN

MISSING IN ACTION

He's late. That's not like him," said Tyler.

Alena checked the clock again. "It's only been an hour. He'll be here."

The *Sea Worthy* was anchored in Gansbaai Harbor, rocking gently in the early morning swells. Around them, the small town was coming to life. Cage-diving boats and fishing boats were getting ready for a busy day. A few cars and delivery trucks were moving on the streets that fronted the harbor. The twins were finishing breakfast on deck. Brutus was suspiciously eyeing a gull that had landed on the railing nearby. The birds occasionally made the small dog a target for…well, you can use your imagination.

The team had returned shaken, but safe, from their encounter with the giant hovercraft and its deadly spawn of go-fast boats. Considering the threat on their lives, and Arky's fate, Tyler had decided to move the *Sea Worthy* from the exposed area near Danger Point to the protection of the harbor. They all agreed to meet the next morning to talk and plan, and Jakob had left.

Now he was late.

"I have a bad feeling about this," said Tyler. "I'm going to go look for him."

Alena was uncomfortable with Tyler leaving, but was also worried about Jakob. She turned to her laptop computer. "I'll finish my report for the Foundation. Take your satellite phone in case he shows up while you're gone," she told her brother.

Tyler helped Brutus into the dingy and putt-putted over to the dock, where he rented a car for the short trip to the Whalesong Lodge in nearby De Kelders where Jakob was staying.

As Tyler left the harbor, a long, low boat quietly pulled in, anchoring out of sight of the *Sea Worthy*.

* * * * *

Jakob was not in his room at the Whalesong Lodge, and the manager said he hadn't seen him come in last night. "Though I think his car's in the lot."

Outside, Brutus was standing at alert near one of the cars. He was softly whining.

"What is it boy?" Tyler asked.

Brutus's ears were flattened back and he was looking underneath the car. Tyler kneeled down to look. Something glinted by the front wheel. It was a pair of glasses.

Tyler grabbed them and stood up. "Good boy," he said to Brutus. He looked carefully at the glasses. He was sure they were Jakob's. One of the lenses was cracked where the frame had been bent.

Just then his phone rang. He looked at the caller ID. "Alena?" he said into the phone.

He heard a man's loud voice in the background, followed by Alena's urgent voice.

"Tyler!" she cried.

Then he heard a crack, as though the phone had been dropped. Or thrown.

Then nothing.

Tyler drove as fast as the law allowed. Still, the trip back to Gansbaai seemed to take forever. He and Brutus jumped into the dingy. He started the motor and aimed for the *Sea Worthy*.

"Alena," he said as they scrambled aboard. "Alena!"

He rushed across the deck of the *Sea Worthy* and jumped down the stairs to the lounge.

"Alena—" He stopped in his tracks.

The lounge was a mess. Furniture was overturned; equipment was scattered around. The box of *Walker's Stem Ginger Biscuits* had tipped over and crumbs were strewn across the floor.

Tyler searched from bow to stern.

There was nothing. No one.

First Jakob, now Alena. Gone. Who had taken them? And where?

It wasn't hard for him to guess.

EIGHT

POISON FLOWER

They had taken her by surprise. Alena had had time to speed dial Tyler and tip over some furniture—and sacrifice their favorite cookies—so that her brother would know something had gone wrong if she didn't reach him by phone. Her biggest fear at the time was that they'd leave someone behind for Tyler. But the pirates were in a hurry. Without a word, they forced her into the go-fast boat's forward hold, bolted the door, and left the harbor.

The dark hold reeked of fish. When her eyes adjusted to the light seeping in from blacked-out portholes, she looked around. The forward section of the boat had been gutted. There was a cargo lift and a winch wound with steel cable. Large storage bins lined the bulkheads.

Curious, Alena opened one. She staggered back and lost her footing, falling heavily onto the deck, which was slick with scales and slime.

The bin was packed solid with shark fins!

So this is how they catch the sharks, she thought.

She did the dreadful math: four go-fast boats, just like this one. Killing sharks. Day after day.

The boat picked up speed and was soon slamming against the swells in the open ocean. Heading to the mother ship with its cruel cargo.

The girl hardly noticed. Tears were streaming down her face,

blurring her vision.

Some time later, the boat stopped. Alena could hear laughter and shouts outside. Then the motor and gears began grinding, and the deck over her head opened up like a big box. They were in the cavernous hold of the mother ship. She remembered Tyler's explanation that the hovercraft was built to lower its huge loading door after the ship had pulled onto land. This one had obviously been modified so the door could open in water, letting the go-fast boats come and go, and then pump the water out.

The crew began unloading the shark fins.

Alena was taken to a large room in the command center. A few minutes later the pirate crew came in. Some of the men stared at the young girl with curiosity. One winked and gave here a creepy leer. A few talked quietly. They all seemed to be waiting for something.

They were a mixed bunch: short, tall, thin, fat, ponytails, shaved heads, beards, mustaches, light-skinned and dark. The only thing they seemed to have in common was a tattoo. On the side of each neck—except where covered by an unruly beard—were the symbols:

$$毒花$$

They looked Chinese to Alena. They were the same symbols she had seen on the man's uniform during the sea chase.

Deciding to take matters into her own hands, and trying hard not to appear afraid, she pointed to the symbols on one of the pirates.

"What is that?" she asked.

The man grunted something in a language she didn't understand and turned away.

"What you say?" another crewmember said in English.

Alena recognized him as the man who had fired the rocket that had brought Arky down. If possible, she found she disliked him even more than the others. But she knew she would gain nothing by showing it, so she kept her voice calm. "What does that mean?"

"*Doo hwa.* It means—" He searched for the right words. "It means Poison Flower. It means we belong Poison Flower."

"You mean you're all crewmembers on this ship? The *Poison Flower*?"

He looked confused. "No. No ship. We belong *Doo hwa.* Poison Flower."

"I think what you mean is—"

"What he said is exactly what he means," came a voice behind her.

Alena whirled and found herself staring at a beautiful woman dressed in a long, flowing dress.

"They all belong to me. I am Poison Flower."

NINE

A RESCUE PLAN

Tyler was waiting. And worrying. And thinking.

The waiting was the hardest part.

Alena had never been in so much trouble. Dangerous dives, sure. But they'd always been together. They were a team. Each one was there to help the other. Tough tests at school. Yeah. But they were great study partners. He drilled her on what she didn't know and vice-versa. Well, maybe she helped him a little more than he helped her. But, the thing was, they were in it together.

Until now.

Would the pirates communicate? Would they bargain? What was Alena going through? When would he see her again? His questions were interrupted by the sound of the computer beeping. It began downloading the files he had requested from the Foundation.

The waiting was over. Now the work began.

Tyler opened a file and found himself looking at 3-D drawings of a *Zubr* hovercraft. He could rotate, pan, and scale the drawings, checking out the inner workings of the ship in perfect detail from any angle. Along with the 3-D drawings were plans of the ship's mechanical and electrical systems.

He studied the files and plans for hours, making lots of notes. He talked out the complex ideas with Brutus—a habit he had when he

was trying to solve hard problems. And this was one of the hardest he'd ever tried to solve: it might mean Alena's life.

He forgot the time. He forgot his dinner.

He even forgot the dog's dinner.

Brutus forgave him. He seemed to know how important this was.

Finally, after he'd done all he could, Tyler closed the files. He smiled for the first time in hours. "Come on Brutus. Here's how we're going to do this..." He headed for the A.I. lab, grabbing the TV remote control on his way.

Brutus perked up his ears and wagged his tail as Tyler explained the plan.

Ten

Pure Poison

"Are you worried?" The woman looked at Alena. Her eyes had all the warmth of a glacier.

They were in the communication center, surrounded by speakers, screens, dials, and buttons. A crewman wearing headphones was monitoring radio signals. Another was watching satellite images. Like a spider in the center of its web, Poison Flower sat in the middle of it all, in a comfortable chair she could raise, tilt, and turn with the push of a button.

Alena was seated nearby. "Should I be worried?"

"You were a bit of a problem. Not so much now," said Poison Flower. "We have your Zulu friend aboard."

Alena couldn't hide her gasp of surprise.

"That's right. Mr. Bheka was far too trusting. He wanted to help a poor, lost little Chinese lady." She smiled sweetly. "I'm told you gave my men some trouble. But here you are." She seemed very pleased with herself.

"Haven't you forgotten something?" Alena said.

"Your darling brother and your little dog?" She gave a sinister laugh. "Whatever will they do? They cannot catch us. And we'll know the moment your ship leaves the harbor."

"I meant the Foundation," Alena said.

Poison Flower looked hard at the girl. "The S.O.S. Foundation?" She turned to one of the crewmen. "Carl. Can you amplify that for us?"

The man turned a dial and Alena heard the familiar voice of the Foundation's Chief Security Officer. *"We're trying to find the owners to open negotiations with them, Tyler. But it may be awhile before—"*

Then she heard Tyler's voice: *"But time might be running out. Isn't there something more we can do?"*

Alena felt a small knot of fear in her stomach. If they had the power to spy on the Foundation's communications with Tyler, then Alena knew she was in real danger.

"That's enough." The voices stopped. "Now are you worried?" Poison Flower said.

Alena put on a brave face. "Not in the least."

"You should be. Now off you go." She signaled one of the crewmen who took Alena to a nearby cabin and locked her in.

She had never felt more alone.

ELEVEN

THE HUNT

It was near dawn, the time when sea lions along the coast left the shallow water shelter of their islands and rocks to hunt for food. Knowing there was safety in numbers, they set out in great packs. Thousands bunched together, heading for the open ocean.

On the way back, it was different. There were some who took longer to catch breakfast than others. They were the stragglers. The ones hunted by sharks.

This morning, however, the sharks were hunted as well.

* * * * *

"Everything set?" Poison Flower asked.

She was supervising the launch from the lead go-fast boat inside the loading dock. The crewmen shouted and pumped their fists in the air, ready to go. There was a lot of money to be made.

Using her headset microphone, Poison Flower talked to the remaining crewmen in the communication center. "Any traffic? Any problems?"

"Just a pod of whales a few minutes ago. Nothing else." Several species of cetaceans came to nearby Mossel Bay each year to give birth to their young. Humpbacks, orcas, and Southern Wright whales were common in the area.

"Any new messages from the Foundation or the little Worthy boy?" she asked.

"The boy told them he would wait at Gansbaai," replied a crewman. "Maybe he expects to hear from you?"

"He'll have a long wait," she said. "Let's go." She signaled the waiting crews.

The massive loading door opened. Commands were shouted. Instructions given. One by one, the go-fast boats left the mother ship and picked up speed, heading for the killing zone.

When the last one had left, pumps started up, expelling the seawater. The door slowly groaned closed. Lights in the interior of the loading area went dark.

Two black-suited figures swam inside just before the door sealed shut. One of the figures turned on a narrow-beam flashlight.

The loading area was deserted as they emerged from the water. They moved quietly to a ladder leading up to a walkway.

One of the figures wore a black wetsuit, a mask, and a compact rebreather unit that gave off no bubbles to give away their presence. The other figure was much smaller, wore four little fins, and a smaller rebreather unit. The face behind the custom-made mask still looked a little like a crazy Siamese cat.

Tyler helped Brutus up the ladder and helped him off with the gear.

The *Nous Venons* was just below the surface and next to the hull of the huge ship, its autopilot keeping it in place.

The trip from Gansbaai to the *Zubr* had been made in orca-mode: an operation that quieted the sub's engine noises. It couldn't go as fast, but it was virtually silent. And the sub's underwater speakers transmitted the sounds of a pod of whales—orcas—that would confuse any vessel listening, such as the mother ship.

Tyler silently made his way to a large electronic panel. He had copied the ship's plans onto his palm computer. He opened the panel. Referring to the drawings in his computer, it only took him a few minutes to find the circuits he was looking for. He made several adjustments.

Then it was time to find Alena and Jakob.

TWELVE

MIXED MESSAGES

Tyler and Brutus made their way along deserted passageways.

The door into the communication center was open and Tyler paused, carefully peeking around the corner. Two crewmembers were there. They were supposed to be monitoring radio and satellite traffic, but they must have become bored because their headphones were sitting on the counter and they were playing a card game of some kind. Tyler took a deep breath and continued.

He figured Alena wouldn't be too far away. He and Brutus crept past the open door and continued down the passageway, trying the handles on the doors they passed. They were all locked. He signaled Brutus.

The terrier sniffed at one of the doors, then scratched at it with his nails. There was movement on the other side.

"Alena?" Tyler whispered.

"Tyler!" came the answering whisper.

"Hold on a second." Tyler pulled out some special tools and, moments later, the door swung open.

Alena was laughing and crying as she hugged her brother. Brutus was bouncing around in joy at their feet.

"We're not out of this yet," Tyler warned.

"They've got Jakob next door," Alena said. "We've been tapping on the bulkhead to keep each other's spirits up."

"Let's get him."

A short time later, the team was reunited.

The plan was working perfectly so far. Of course, that's when things started going wrong.

The speakers had been turned up in the communication center and the crewmen were listening in confusion.

"We're trying to find the owners to open negotiations with them, Tyler. But it may be awhile before—"

Then came Tyler's voice: *"But time might be running out. Isn't there something more we can do?"*

"That sounds familiar," said one crewman.

As they listened, they realized they were hearing exactly the same message they'd heard earlier. It was repeating, word for word. They didn't know that Tyler had edited several long conversations with the Foundation into a long, repeating loop that the Foundation's satellites then transmitted, making anyone listening think Tyler was still on the *Sea Worthy* in Gansbaai harbor.

"Something's wrong here," said the other crewman. "You'd better let the Captain know."

The man shuddered. *"You* let her know. *I'll* check our prisoners." He left the room quickly.

The other man picked up a microphone, dreading giving the bad news. "Captain. We've got a problem—"

When he had explained, the enraged screech that came out of the speakers could be heard throughout the command center.

Jakob and the A.I. team were on deck, heading for a ladder, when they were discovered.

"You!" came the shout from behind. "Stop!"

They turned to see a crewman almost upon them, holding a gun.

"Brutus! Gun!" Alena called.

The dog launched himself at the man, grabbing his wrist. The man screamed and dropped the weapon.

Meanwhile, Tyler was talking hurriedly into his Bluetooth headset. "*Nous Venons*. Surface."

Beneath the ocean, the sub rumbled to life and floated to the surface.

While one crewman writhed on the deck, trying to pry the jaws of the dog from his injured arm, the other crewman was running toward them, shouting.

Jakob was moving to intercept him. As the crewman swung his fist, the tall Zula ducked aside and stuck out his foot. The man sprawled headlong onto the deck.

Tyler yelled, "Over the side! Now!"

"Brutus! Let's go!" Alena said. The brave dog loosened his hold on the man's wrist and headed for the side with the rest of his team.

Then, with Tyler carrying Brutus, the team scrambled down the ladder, jumping the last few meters and landing next to the waiting *Nous Venons*.

Thirteen

The Hunters Hunted

Poison Flower was screaming again. Her squadron of go-fast boats was scattered up and down the coast. But, instead of being the hunters, they had become the hunted. Each go-fast boat was surrounded by a flotilla—a small fleet of boats—filled with angry citizens and authorities from Gansbaai and nearby towns. After Tyler had given the Foundation the information, satellites had tracked the go-fast boats from the time they had left the mother ship. Cage-diving companies, commercial fishing companies, even local pleasure boat owners had been secretly notified, and had taken to the water in force.

Poison Flower could now see boats closing in on her. She jammed the throttle forward and the boat headed for the Zub. She and her crew reached the *Zubr* to find a mess. Two of her men were injured. Her prisoners had escaped. Her carefully planned operation was falling apart. She had never been so angry. Ruined by children! she fumed.

In the communication center, she checked satellite images. Dyer Island. Geyser Rock. *There!* She zoomed in. *That submarine! Those children!*

Poison Flower screamed at the crewmen to get ready to launch the powerful hovercraft. She was big into screaming today. Frightened by her anger, her remaining crew rallied and went to work.

Four ten-thousand-horsepower hover engines roared to life, lifting

the boat up on its air cushion. Three forward-thrust engines spun up to fifteen-thousand rpm.

The ship picked up speed and within a minute was skimming across the sea at more than 60 knots.

Poison Flower was hunting revenge.

FOURTEEN

PAYBACK

At the opposite end of the channel between Dyer Island and Geyser Rock, Tyler turned the *Nous Venons* around to face Poison Flower.

He stopped the engines. The sub sat motionless in the water. Unless something happened quickly, the huge hovercraft would ram and sink the small submarine.

The team was crowded together in the conning tower, watching the ship race toward them.

"This is part of the plan, right little brother?" Alena asked. "Right?"

Tyler just grinned and handed Jakob the TV remote control. "You do the honors."

Tyler had rewired the remote control in the A.I. lab, just as he had rewired circuits aboard the *Zubr*.

Jakob's smile lit up his whole face. He pointed the remote control at the hovercraft, now less than half a kilometer away.

He pushed a button.

Aboard the *Zubr*, Poison Flower screamed again. The lights on the communication console were telling her the impossible. The ship's huge loading door was opening while they were traveling at top speed! She stabbed at the controls to close the door. Nothing! She reached for the engine controls. Nothing!

Like a huge mouth, the door gaped open into the on-rushing sea.

Instantly, millions of liters of water gushed into the vast loading area. The ship shuddered violently. It wasn't meant to sustain this much water at once.

The team heard the screaming of metal being wrenched apart, the loud crackling of electrical circuits sparking and shorting out. In less than five seconds the hovercraft went from full speed to a dead stop, and began sinking in the middle of the channel.

The team watched as tiny figures emerged from the command center and scrambled for the side, throwing themselves into the water just before the deck was submerged.

They entered the water on the side nearest Geyser Rock and began frantically swimming toward shore—through water patrolled by the great white sharks.

A little while later, Tyler gave a sigh of relief as Poison Flower and her crewmen scrambled safely ashore onto Geyser Rock.

Alena was still angry and unsettled at her treatment aboard the hovercraft. "Maybe it would have been better if the great whites had spotted them first."

Tyler smiled. "No. She'll be arrested along with all her crew. The killing is over. The boat isn't a threat anymore."

Just then, they heard a disgusted scream echoing across the water.

"And Poison Flower will be enjoying the company—and the smell—of fifty-thousand Cape fur seals until the authorities can get to them," Tyler added with a grin.

Jakob smiled.

Alena laughed out loud.

Brutus yipped and yapped, bouncing up and down in excitement.

Then Tyler turned the *Nous Venons* around and headed back to safe harbor.

FIFTEEN

REWARDS

Shafts of sunlight streamed down through the blue-green water. Two great whites swam majestically near some rocky outcroppings.

In her scuba gear, Alena was enraptured as she watched the beautiful creatures. Next to her, Tyler was filming. The more the world knew about these magnificent animals, the safer they would be. The rest of the countries in the world would outlaw their senseless killing. Laws would be enforced. Shark fin soup would be taken off the menus in restaurants.

Tyler looked at his sister and smiled.

She smiled back.

Just then their masks pulsed red and they heard "*AI Code Red. This is not a drill. Repeat. This is not a drill. This is an AI Code Red.*"

The nearby sharks paid no attention.

The twins headed for the surface.

Nous venons! Alena said to herself. *We're coming!*

GLOSSARY

Autonomous
Independent, self-directed.

Bluetooth
A short-range radio technology for Internet and mobile devices, such as phones, which simplifies hands-free.

GPS
An abbreviation of Global Positioning System. A system of satellites, computers, and receivers that is able to determine the latitude and longitude of a receiver on Earth by calculating the time difference for signals from different satellites to reach the receiver.

Hovercraft
A usually propeller-driven vehicle designed for traveling over land or water on a supportive cushion of slowly moving, low-pressure air.

Hydroplane
A light, high-powered boat, especially one with hydrofoils or a stepped bottom, designed to plane along the surface of the water at very high speeds. The Sea Worthy was designed by the S.O.S. Foundation with wings and a tail that can be unfolded so the boat can be used as an airplane.

Kilometer
A unit of length in the metric system. A meter is equal to 39.37 inches. A kilometer is 1000 meters, equal to 3280.8 feet or 0.621 mile. It is abbreviated: km.

LED
Light-emitting diode: a semiconductor diode that emits light when conducting current and is used in electronic equipment, esp. for displaying readings on digital watches, calculators, etc.

Microscope

An optical instrument having a magnifying lens for inspecting objects too small to be seen in detail by the unaided eye. The scanning electron microscope aboard the Sea Worthy is a microscope that moves a narrowly focused beam of electrons across an object and detects the patterns. From these patterns a three-dimensional image of the object is created.

Pinnipeds

Animals belonging to the Pinnipedia, a suborder of carnivorous aquatic mammals that includes the seals, walruses, and similar animals having finlike flippers as organs of locomotion.

Plexiglas

A light, transparent, weather-resistant plastic.

Rebreather Unit

Sometimes called CCUBA – Closed Circuit Underwater Breathing Apparatus. A type of breathing set that provides a breathing gas containing oxygen and recycles exhaled gas. This recycling reduces the volume of breathing gas used, making a rebreather lighter and more compact than SCUBA.

Reconnaissance

An inspection or exploration of an area.

Satellite

A device designed to be launched into orbit around the earth, another planet, the sun, etc. Communication satellites are used to receive and transmit information.

Scuba

An abbreviation of Self-Contained Underwater Breathing Apparatus. A portable breathing device for free-swimming divers, consisting of a mouthpiece joined by hoses to one or two tanks of compressed air that are strapped on the back.

Submarine

A vessel that can be submerged and navigated under water.

Zulu

A member of the Nguni people living mainly in Natal, Republic of South Africa.

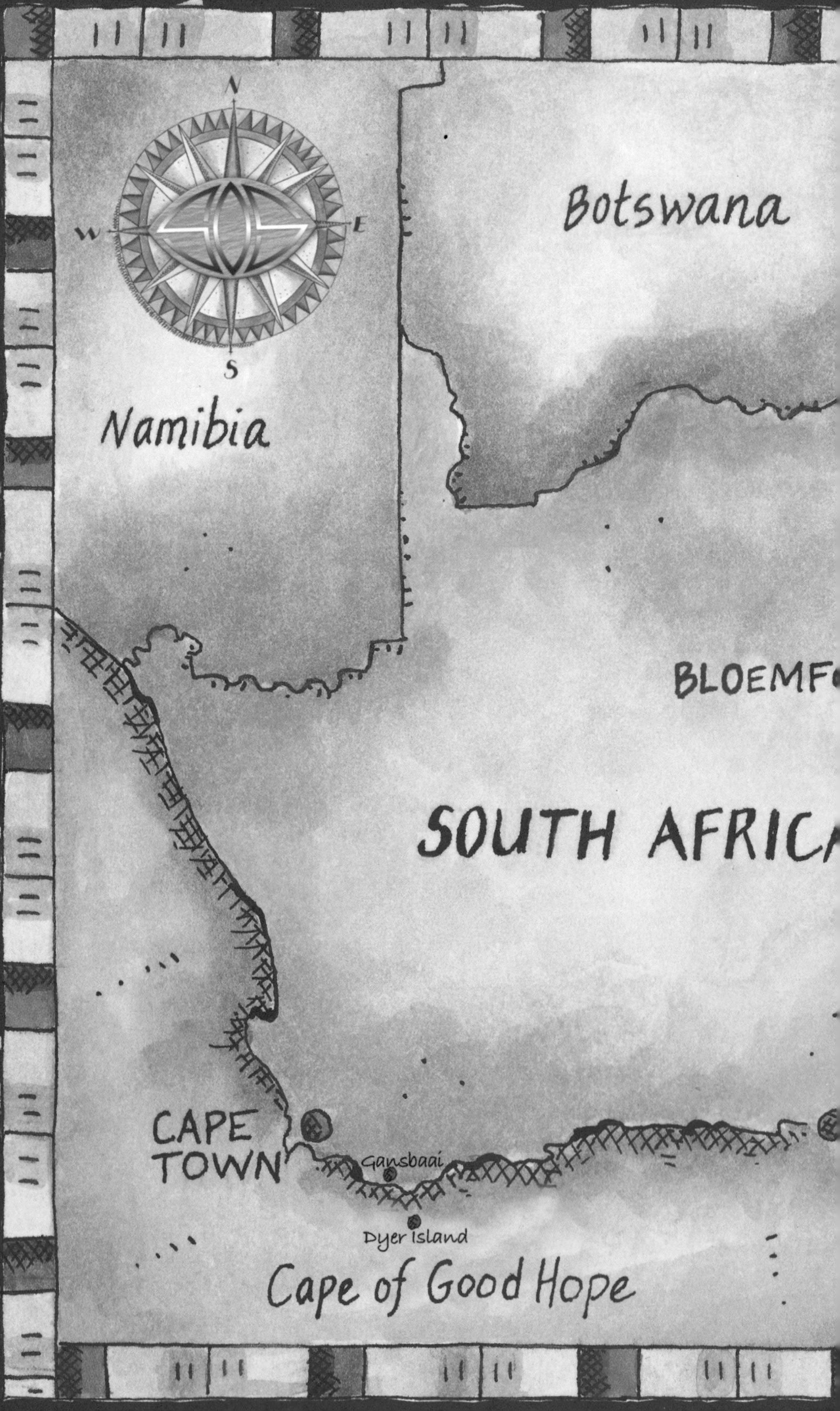
N
W
E
S
Botswana
Namibia
BLOEMF
SOUTH AFRIC
CAPE
TOWN
Gansbaai
Dyer Island
Cape of Good Hope